Samuel's Choice

RICHARD BERLETH

illustrated by JAMES WATLING

ALBERT WHITMAN & COMPANY
CHICAGO, ILLINOIS

FOR HANNA—RB
FOR DŌ—JW

Library of Congress Cataloging-in-Publication Data

Berleth, Richard J.
Samuel's choice/Richard Berleth;
illustrated by James Watling.
p. cm.
Summary: Samuel, a fourteen-year-old slave in Brooklyn
in 1776, faces a difficult choice when the fighting
between the British and the colonists reaches his
doorstep and only he can help the rebels.
1. Long Island, Battle of, 1776—Juvenile fiction.
[1. Long Island, Battle of, 1776—Fiction. 2. United
States—History—Revolution, 1775–1783—Campaigns—
Fiction. 3. Afro-Americans—Fiction.] I. Watling,
James, ill. II. Title.
PZ7.B4533Sam   1990   89-77186
[Fic]-dc20   CIP
                                                    AC

Text copyright © 1990 by Richard J. Berleth
Illustrations copyright © 1990 by James Watling
Hardcover edition first published in the United States of
America in 1990 by Albert Whitman & Company
Paperback edition first published in the United States of
America in 2012 by Albert Whitman & Company
ISBN 978-0-8075-7219-1 (paperback)

Printed in China
15 14 13 12 11 T&N 24 23 22 21 20

For more information about Albert Whitman & Company,
visit our website at www.albertwhitman.com.

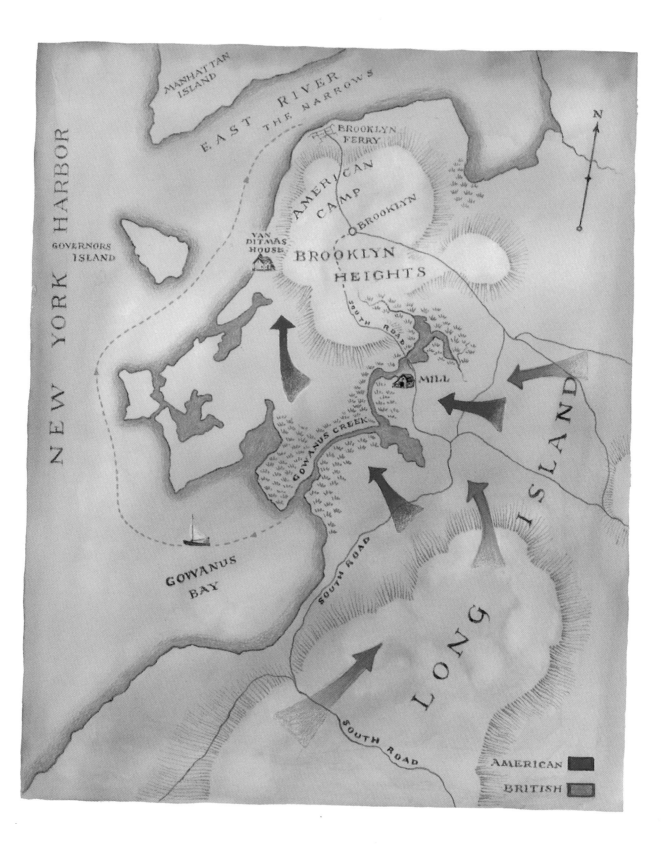

MY MASTER, ISAAC VAN DITMAS, was a very rich farmer. In my fourteenth year, he bought me from his old aunt in Flushing and took me from my parents to work as a slave in his flour mill on Gowanus Creek in Brooklyn. That same time he bought Sana Williams, Toby, and others to keep the gardens and kitchen of his big house on New York Harbor.

At the end of Long Island, the Heights of Brooklyn overlooked the East River and Manhattan Island. To the south lay the town of Brooklyn; it was only a small one in those days. The long South Road ran across Long Island's hills, through fields of wheat and rye, connecting Brooklyn town with the Narrows at the entrance to New York Harbor.

Gowanus Creek, where the flour mill stood, wound out of this harbor into the green fields and lost itself in ponds and marshes. On a summer evening, the mosquitoes rose like clouds from still waters and settled, stinging, on our bare arms and necks.

Farmer Isaac was a strict man. Our day began at sunrise and ended when the light faded. Round and round the great stone wheel rolled and rumbled all day long, driven by tides flowing in and out of the creek. We ground wheat to make bread at the mill. We shoveled the flour into bags, and loaded the bags into boats, to be brought to bakers in Manhattan. But little bread we ever saw. Van Ditmas was a stingy man. Many nights I went to bed with my stomach growling and only the taste of the raw flour on my lips.

When Farmer Isaac saw that I had grown strong and could row a boat well, he taught me about the currents that flow between Brooklyn and Manhattan, about setting a sail and holding a course. I was to row Mrs. van Ditmas and her daughters over to Manhattan, or down the Brooklyn shore to Staten Island across the harbor. Isaac shook me by the collar and warned me never to row or sail except where he sent me. I was his property, according to the laws of the Crown Colony, and he could do what he wanted with me.

Work you do not choose to do is always tiring. And even the house slaves, who labored in Farmer Isaac's kitchen, got little sleep and less food. Whenever I felt the fresh sea breeze on my face, I would look up at the gulls flying where they pleased and I would dream. I wondered how it was to be free like them, to go where I wanted.

America, being ruled by the king of England, was not a separate country. And these were troubled times in all the colonies. The night came when Manhattan Island was lit up like daytime with a hundred bonfires. We gathered on the steps of the great house and heard the cheers and shouts echo over the water. Then came the sound of drums and fifes, songs and cannon firing.

"What's all that racket over there?" Sana asked.

"That's the sound of people going free," old Toby answered. "Free from the king of England. Free from the likes of van Ditmas."

"How they get free, Toby?"

"Why they up and said they was free, girl, and wrote those words down on paper."

Sana laughed. "You gotta do more than say you're free. That king and Isaac, do they care what anybody say?"

What was it, I wondered, that made people think they could change their lives? They called their freedom "liberty," and they marched through Brooklyn town cheering for that liberty.

When the Sons of Liberty finally came, waving their flags, Isaac locked us in the house.

In the kitchen, the servants argued. "Liberty ain't for Africans," one said. "And it got nothin' to do with us," another said.

But Sana just shook her head. She was fifteen and had been to church school. She could write her name and could read. "Nobody here's gonna be free unless they take the risk. Open your eyes! War is coming to Brooklyn 'tween that English king and those Sons of Liberty. We can't say who'll win. We can't say how many black slaves are ever gonna get free. But one thing is sure—it's never gonna happen under Isaac van Ditmas."

The talk made my head spin. One moment it seemed to offer hope, and then the arguments turned and I didn't feel hope anymore. One day Liberty men nailed a proclamation to a tree by the South Road. But before anyone could tell me what it said, Isaac came and tore it down and stamped on it in the dust. That was the day Sana promised she would teach me to read. "That writing, Samuel," she said later, "was the Declaration of Independence, made by Thomas Jefferson in the Congress at Philadelphia."

So the summer of 1776, my fourteenth one, passed on. Day by day, my back and arms grew stronger with hard work. More than once I looked up from filling flour sacks to find a cool jar of buttermilk left by Sana. Then I'd drink the milk and fill the empty jar with flour. When she fetched the jar back, she would hide it. One day I asked what she wanted with so much flour. She just smiled and said, "That flour will be bread for our freedom day."

While I sailed on Farmer Isaac's errands or loaded sacks of flour, the war crept towards Brooklyn. On a fine morning we woke in the slave quarters to the thunder of great guns out in the harbor. I ran up to the house. Sana just kept on calmly with her work. "Washington's come to New York," she said, grinning. "Those are guns out of Governors Island practicing to scare off the British."

Well, the guns sure scared off Farmer Isaac. After Washington arrived, he and Mrs. van Ditmas never crossed to Manhattan again. I hoisted the sail of my boat to carry the farmer's wife and daughters, with all their trunks, to an old uncle's house on Staten Island.

And there on Staten Island, I saw them. The king's army had come from across the sea and on the hillside meadows had pitched its tents by the thousands. The sun glinted on rows of brass cannon and bayonets. Redcoats came down from the hills. They spread over the green grass like streams of blood, and they sat in barges and were rowed across to the Brooklyn shore. A barge passed nearby. We saw the smiling, sunburned faces of the soldiers. "Hurrah!" they cheered, and the van Ditmas girls waved and giggled.

Back in the kitchen of the big house, I told what I had seen.

"Those great ships have hundreds of cannon," Toby said.

"There's got to be thousands of Redcoats," somebody else said, "and they gonna whip these Liberty Boys but good."

"General Washington will find a way," Sana said, but her eyes held back tears. "It can't just end like this!"

Old Toby put an arm around her. "Trouble is, dear, it can. These Americans are settin' up to fight their king, and that means all the king's ships, and men, and cannon."

"No business for us black slaves, I'm tellin' you," said Joseph Martin.

"Not with Isaac down so hard on the Liberty Boys," Loretta added.

It seemed to me the slaves were right. I could not think how the ordinary Americans I had seen, fresh from their farms and shops, could ever drive away an army of real soldiers.

The next day, while I loaded sacks into a wagon, I heard the sound of fifes and drums. Southwards, along the road past the mill, came a hundred of Washington's recruits, their feet shuffling in the dust. An American officer rode beside them on a gray farmhorse.

"Captain!" Sana called to him. "Thousands of them are landing down the shore!"

"We know that, girl," he called back. "Don't worry, we'll handle them lobster backs. General Washington himself is coming over to Brooklyn." But the men marching past us didn't look so sure. Many seemed frightened. Some were barefoot. Some looked hungry and sick. Their flags drooped. As they passed, Sana read the names of the colonies embroidered on their banners: Pennsylvania, Delaware, Maryland, Rhode Island. They had come from far away to a strange place.

Farmer Isaac stood by the fence, puffing on his pipe. "You be quiet, girl. This isn't no fight of yours. If them fools want to break the king's law, they can get themselves killed with no help from my slaves."

Sana shook her head. I knew she felt sorry for the ragged men and boys marching past. Maybe they were not fighting for her liberty. Not yet. But freedom had to start somewhere. That summer it was starting in Brooklyn.

When the officer was gone, and Isaac, too, one of his men stopped by the wagon. He just stood there and stared at me.

"You thirsty?" I asked him. He nodded and held his empty canteen upside down. I snatched my jug of buttermilk out of the wagon and poured it into the canteen. The boy took a long drink.

"Thanks," he said. "My name's Nathaniel. Joined up at Boston on my fourteenth birthday."

"You know how to shoot that thing?" I asked, pointing at his musket.

"Think so," he muttered. "Shot it yesterday in camp."

"You scared?" I asked him.

"No, I ain't," he said.

"Well, you oughta be," I told him.

All day long the guns crashed and boomed on the Long Island hills. While the mill wheel rumbled and ground, soldiers rushed down the South Road.

Suddenly there was shouting. A soldier appeared in the doorway. "The British are coming!" he cried. "The Americans are running!"

The road filled with crowds of American soldiers, now running north along the road, back toward Washington's lines. Tired, frightened people. Most were sopping wet. Where they stopped to rest, the dust turned to mud under their feet.

Cannonballs were whizzing through the air. One crashed through the roof of the mill. Farmer Isaac was nowhere to be seen. Sana knelt by someone who had fallen beside the road. She tied a strip of petticoat around a bloody gash in his leg. He was soaked and shaking. When I looked at his face, I saw that he was Nathaniel, the boy with the empty canteen.

"Stop staring," Sana shouted at me. "He's trembling. Wrap him in them empty sacks." Nathaniel told us how he swam across Gowanus Creek to escape from the British. But the tide was rising fast. Dozens of Americans were wounded and many couldn't swim. The army was trapped without boats in the swamps around the creek. Some were still fighting, but lots of soldiers were being shot like ducks in the marshes. Washington's men needed help badly.

Sana's eyes pleaded with me. She knew I tied my boat in the reeds along the creek. Her look said, "It's up to you, Samuel."

Nathaniel groaned. The small red spot on his bandage had begun to spread. Toby had come and was kneeling beside Sana. He shrugged. "You got the boat, Samuel. It's your choice."

Sana and Toby got set to carry Nathaniel up the road into the American lines. Sana caught me looking at the bag on her shoulder.

"That's my freedom flour," she said. "I'm going where I can bake my freedom loaf." A moment later, more soldiers ran between us. When they had passed, Sana, Toby, and Nathaniel were gone.

All at once the road was empty. From away in the distance came the roar of muskets. Isaac van Ditmas was gone. Sana was gone and the soldiers were, too. I was alone.

Was this freedom? I thought about that boy Nathaniel from far away. How a lot more people just like him were trapped in the marshes along the creek. And how Isaac sneered at them, and how the British king from across the waters sent his soldiers to shoot and imprison them. I looked at my hands, grown strong from pulling ropes and oars and sacks. Then I knew my choice. Those hands now were going to pull people, pull them to freedom.

I ran to the creek, pushed the boat out into the rushing tide, and slid the oars into their locks. On the opposite bank Americans were wading in the muddy water up to their waists, shouting for help. In the distance others were holding the British back from the water's edge. Great clouds of gunsmoke rolled over these brave soldiers. When the air cleared, I could see fewer and fewer of them.

As I pulled near, wet and weary men flopped into the boat. Others clung to the sides. "Row, row!" they shouted. I pulled on the oars with all my might. Out we shot into the current. Bullets splashed in the water near us. When we reached the far bank, the men cheered. I turned again into the creek and rowed back for more.

Six times I crossed the creek. Each time the battle grew closer, the fleeing Americans fewer. By now muddy water slopped around my ankles. My back ached from pulling on the oars.

Just as I was raising the sail to race out of the creek, I glimpsed a big man in a blue coat and three-cornered hat alone in the bullreeds. He threw himself into the boat and ordered me to sail for Washington's camp. The British were close behind him. As we fled down the creek into New York Harbor, they fired at us from the banks. When the big man had caught his breath, he pointed up at the sail. Black holes gaped in the canvas.

"Musket balls," he said and winked. "Compliments of General Cornwallis."

As the boat carried us out into the harbor, I steered northward along the Brooklyn shore toward Brooklyn Heights and Washington's camp. I wondered what Farmer Isaac would say about his torn sail. But most of all, I wondered what had happened to Sana and Toby.

My passenger's name was Major Mordecai Gist. He commanded the Maryland soldiers who had held back the British while other Americans escaped. "Oh, what brave boys I lost today," said Major Gist, "and this war has only begun." He asked how I came to be fishing men out of the creek. I told him about Farmer Isaac, Sana, and Nathaniel.

When I tied the boat to the dock below the Heights, Major Gist clapped his hands on my shoulders and looked me in the eyes. "Samuel," he said, "out in that creek you did more than many a free man for your country. I'd take it as a privilege if you'd consent to be my orderly and march beside me. And General Washington may need handy boatmen like you soon enough."

The next day it rained and rained. A thick sea fog covered the land. I looked everywhere for Sana. Many soldiers crowded into the camp, but they could tell me nothing. Alone and frightened, I mended the holes in my sail, pushing the big needle through the canvas, drawing it back again. Then, I heard voices nearby.

Major Gist stood there with an officer in a fine blue uniform. They asked me how deep the water was at this point between Brooklyn and Manhattan. They wanted to know if a British ship could sail between the two places. I told them that most ships could. Only the fog was keeping the British men-of-war from trapping Washington's army on Long Island.

The officer in the blue uniform thanked me. He and Major Gist walked away, looking thoughtful.

The next day the heavy rains continued. I spread the sail over the boat and slept snug and dry. Then I heard the voice I missed more than any in the world calling, "Samuel, Samuel Abraham!" Sana had found me! It was not a dream. "You chose, Samuel," she said. "You did it right. You chose our new country." From under her cloak she took a hot, steaming loaf wrapped in a napkin—her freedom bread, the sweetest I ever tasted. While we ate, she told me that Toby and Nathaniel were safe.

But this new country was in danger. Major Gist came to me again and explained that every boat was needed to carry Washington's army from Brooklyn to Manhattan. The army had to retreat that night. I was going to help save the army with Farmer Isaac's boat. Wouldn't he be surprised?

On the night that General Washington's army left Brooklyn, the worst storm I'd ever seen blew in from the Northeast. The wind howled. It drove the rain, stinging, into our eyes. It shook buildings and knocked down chimneys. And it whipped the water at Brooklyn Ferry into a sea of foam.

Down from the Heights in file marched Washington's army. The men entered the boats Major Gist and others had gathered at the ferry landing.

"What we need is a rope to cling to," someone said in the dark. "A rope stretching from here to Manhattan to guide us against the wind and current."

"There's rope here in the shipyard," a soldier remembered. "Buoys to float the rope across, too. But who can cross this flood in the dark?"

"Can you do it, Samuel?" Major Gist asked. "Can you get across with the rope?"

"I can do it, Major," I shouted, the wind tearing the words out of my mouth. But I wasn't sure. Even if the rope were fed out from shore slowly, the sail might split or the rope might tear down the mast. But the British ships were sure to force their way between Brooklyn and Manhattan. I had to try.

When the rope was ready, I tied it to the foot of the mast. Sana jumped into the boat. I shouted at her to stay behind, but she wouldn't move. There was no time to lose. I shoved off into the swirling current.

My only hope was to let the shore current carry me out into midstream, and then, as the wind and tide thrust the boat toward the other shore, raise the sail and race for the Manhattan landing.

Fighting the rudder, I heard Sana's voice in my ear. "Will we make it, Samuel?" Water crashed over the side. Sana was bailing as fast as she could. "I can't swim, Samuel!" she cried into the wind. We were halfway across to Manhattan, and the boat was filling with sea. The gale was spinning us around. The rope was pulling us backward. I heaved at the sail, praying the mending wouldn't tear.

Then, as the sail filled, the boom swung around with a crack, and we were darting forward at last. On the Manhattan landing, by lantern light, we could see people waiting. Over the roar of the storm, we heard them cheering us on. But Isaac's boat was sinking. The rope was tearing the mast out of the bottom. With a terrible crash, the mast broke and was carried over the side. A second later the bow smashed into the side of a wharf, and I found myself in the water swimming with one arm, clinging to Sana with the other.

We stumbled ashore on Manhattan Island, where kind people wrapped us in blankets. They were smiling—the rope was across! The boats full of Washington's soldiers would follow. We had done it, together.

All through the night Washington's men followed that rope, boat after boat, across the water. In the stormy darkness, every soldier escaped from Long Island.

And so the fight for freedom would go on. It would take many long years before we would beat the British king, but never again did I wonder what freedom was, or what it cost. It was people pulling together. It was strong hands helping. It was one person caring about another.

And where was Washington? Many times that night Sana and I hoped to see him.

"Why, Samuel," Major Gist told us later, "he was that officer in the blue coat who asked you how deep the water was between Brooklyn and Manhattan. Last night the general arrested a farmer in Brooklyn for helping the British. That farmer, Isaac van Ditmas, turned all of his property over to the Army of the Continental Congress in exchange for his freedom. It seems now that you and Sana have no master."

From that day forward, we and Isaac's other slaves were to be citizens of a new nation.

HISTORICAL NOTE: The Battle of Long Island was George Washington's first battle in the American War for Independence. It was a defeat. From Brooklyn, General Washington retreated to Manhattan, then to New Jersey, and in the last month of 1776, he crossed the Delaware River into Pennsylvania. Thus ended one of the longer and more bitter retreats in American history. On the day after Christmas, Washington crossed the icy Delaware once more into New Jersey. There, at Trenton and again at Princeton, his soldiers (many of whom had escaped from Brooklyn) defeated their enemy. In 1781, General Cornwallis finally surrendered at Yorktown. The British troops who fired on Samuel at Gowanus Creek on August 27th, 1776, were commanded by General Cornwallis.

Major Mordecai Gist led the Maryland state troops in the Battle of Long Island. He and Isaac van Ditmas are historical figures (although the arrest of van Ditmas did not actually occur). Samuel Abraham and Sana Williams are fictional, but modeled on the many nameless people of Brooklyn, slave and free, who made Washington's escape possible.